Barnaby's Surprise

illustrated by

Anna Currey

Designed by Zena Flax

Printed and bound in Belgium by Proost
for the publishers Piccadilly Press Ltd.,
5 Castle Road, London NW1 8PR

ISBN: 1 85340 475 6 paperback
1 85340 102 1 hardback

3 5 7 9 10 8 6 4 2

Set in Palatino

A catalogue record for this book is available from the British Library

Anna Currey lives in Corsham, Wiltshire, surrounded by loads of animals.
She has illustrated a number of books, but this is her first for Piccadilly Press.

Barnaby's Surprise

illustrated by

Anna Currey

PICCADILLY PRESS • LONDON

There was nothing special in Barnaby's post that morning, only bills and more bills.

"I'm the saddest rabbit in the whole world," he said.

BURROW REPAIRS
ACCOUNT DUE
BILL FOR DELIVERY OF CARROTS
INLAND REVENUE
PRIVATE

Usually he shared his breakfast with Sid and Samantha, but this morning he didn't come to the window.

"He needs cheering up," said Sid. "But all his friends are busy."

Deep in the woods
the squirrels were
feeling very excited.
"Which do you think
is the nicest - yellow
or blue or red?"
asked Simon.

Barnaby's beautiful
(but rather vain) sisters
were making themselves
even more glamorous
than usual.

The badger family was
busy baking something
extra delicious.

By the river the otters were concentrating on their wrapping paper and ribbons.

At the pond
the frogs were mixing
the most wonderful
cocktails.

The pheasants were carrying messages to and fro.

The mice
in the swamp
were trying
to harmonize.

MAP
MAP

Suddenly, the deer came bounding out of the forest in their best costumes.

Everyone started
to gather in
the clearing.

It was a
surprise party!

TO BARNABY
AY BARNABY
HAPPY BIRTHDAY TO YOU
HAPPY BIRTHDAY TO YOU

Happy birthday,
Barnaby - the happiest rabbit
in the whole world.